DEAR POLTERGEIST

Princess Isobella's being haunted by a poltergeist called Pandora!

Linda Hoy has written fifteen books for young people, including *United on Vacation* and *Haddock 'n' Chips* (Winner of the Sheffield Children's Book Award). She also writes plays and poetry, and visits schools, where she helps children with writing their own stories.

Linda enjoys listening to live music, especially rock bands. She likes walking, cycling, travelling and scoffing her favourite foods – prawn curry and vanilla slices. She lives in Sheffield with her mountain bike.

Books by the same author

Emmeline Pankhurst

Haddock 'n' Chips

Nightmare Express

Nightmare Park

Ring of Death

United on Vacation

Your Friend, Rebecca

Dear Poltergeist

LINDA HOY

Illustrations by

TONY KENYON

WALKER BOOKS
AND SUBSIDIARIES
LONDON · BOSTON · SYDNEY

For Claire

First published 1996 by Walker Books Ltd
87 Vauxhall Walk, London SE11 5HJ

This edition published 2000

2 4 6 8 10 9 7 5 3 1

Text © 1996 Linda Hoy
Illustrations © 1996 Tony Kenyon

The right of Linda Hoy to be identified as author
of this work has been asserted by her in accordance with the
Copyright, Designs and Patents Act 1988.

This book has been typeset in Plantin.

Printed and bound in Great Britain by
The Guernsey Press Co. Ltd

British Library Cataloguing in Publication Data
A catalogue record for this book is
available from the British Library.

ISBN 0-7445-7815-9

J137,951

E5.36

Contents

Chapter 1

The day I first met the poltergeist was the day I got my big toe stuck inside the tap. Not the water tap – one of the milkshake dispensers that stand beside my bath.

Lying back in the bubbles, I reached out my big toe and pressed the CHOCOLATE button. The dispenser made a gurgling sound but no milkshake appeared. I pressed again. It spluttered. I thought the milkshake might be stuck so I pushed my big toe up inside the tap and wiggled it about. Then the tap hissed. It seemed to take a long, deep breath before it sucked my toe inside.

"Ouch!" I shouted. "Stop it!" I don't normally talk to taps but, there again, they don't normally suck my toes.

The tap pulled and bit my toe as tightly as a puppy with a stick.

"*Ouch!*"

I splashed my arm out through the clouds of bubble bath. I reached for my mobile phone and pressed S for Service. "Help!" I shouted.

That's when the next strange thing happened.

Normally, at the other end of the phone, I hear one of the servants. "Yes, Your Royal Highness," they say. "Of course, Your Royal Highness. It's a pleasure, Your Royal Highness."

This time I heard a girl's voice. She was laughing: "Ha, ha, haaa."

Not a nice, pleasant laugh – a mischievous laugh, as if someone had just played a trick on me. "Ha, ha, haaa."

"Who are you?" I shouted crossly.

Silence.

"Who *are* you?"

The phone seemed to take a long, deep breath just like the milkshake dispenser. I held it away from my face before it could suck my ear inside.

"*Well…?*"

There was a moment's pause. Then the girl's voice said. "My name is Pandora. I'm a poltergeist. I've decided to haunt you."

Then she hung up.

When Pandora told me her name, even though I was lying in my nice warm bath, I felt a big rash of goose pimples rise along my arm.

I remembered where I'd seen her name before.

I was practising my juggling outside in the garden when I lost my stripy ball. It flew into the air and landed on the rockery just behind the waterfall.

"Oh, boozle!" I stamped my foot.

I could have shouted for a servant but I couldn't be bothered. Servants are like slugs in a sleep-walk – slow.

I didn't want to get wet so I searched for the tap to turn off the waterfall. Behind the rocks, I found a little wheel. I rolled up my silken sleeves, then turned the wheel anti-clockwise. Sure enough, the water slowed to a dribble.

I jumped down the rocks to find my ball, but just before I picked it up, something caught my eye. Behind the waterfall was a smooth black stone with letters carved and painted in gold.

They said:

HERE LIES
PANDORA
R.I.P.

I stood and stared. Then I looked all round. There was nobody about. So, why did it say someone was lying there when they obviously weren't? And who would want to lie in a waterfall, anyway?

And then I wondered about the letters: R.I.P...?

Raspberries In the Palace?

Rhubarb In Peanut butter?

Really Interesting Person?

You might have guessed by now that inside the palace gardens, I don't meet many interesting people. I only meet servants. All they say is: "Yes, Your Royal Highness. Of course, Your Royal Highness." And: "It's a pleasure, Your Royal Highness." I never meet anyone that I can have a proper conversation with.

Pandora, I thought, might be a Really Interesting Person and she might like to have a proper conversation and play some interesting games with me.

I didn't realize at the time just how true that was going to be.

Chapter 2

So, Pandora's first idea of an interesting game was to suck my toe inside the tap.

"Ouch!" I yelled. I pressed my finger on the *S* button and kept it there. *"Eeeeeeeooooowwwww! Eeeeeeeooooowwwww!"* the siren wailed downstairs where the servants slug about. The sound was swiftly followed by a clambering of heavy footsteps up the royal stairs.

Then the tap spluttered. It seemed to be spitting out my toe as though it didn't like the taste. Then the tap rasped out the loudest, rudest, most disgusting noise that you have ever heard.

The servants halted in my doorway, their eyes growing round as juggling balls. It wasn't the kind of noise they expected a royal princess to make – even in her private bath.

"Go away, you stupid boozles!" I yelled at them. "I'm all right now."

But I wasn't all right at all.

The next thing that happened was that the

row of dispensers beside my bath started to mix themselves up. When I pressed the button for extra bubble bath, it squirted chocolate milkshake right into my face. I wiped it off with my velvet face cloth, then tried to fill my glass with a nice long drink of fruit juice. Instead, I got a great big mouthful of shampoo.

Ugh!

Next, the electric shampooer started washing my hair with milkshake. I sighed deeply and tried to get another drink. When I pressed RASPBERRY, however, I got exactly what I asked for – another very loud, rude noise.

I took a long deep breath.

Perhaps it was time to climb out.

I stepped from the chocolate foam and wrapped myself in a towel. Then I walked through into my bedroom and sat on the velvet-topped stool in front of my dressing-table.

*"Mirror, mirror on the wall
who's the fairest of them all?"*

I asked. I don't normally talk to mirrors either but someone taught me this rhyme when I was very small and I've been saying it ever since.

Needless to say, the mirror has never answered back.

Anyway, I switched on my electric hairbrush and that's when the next strange thing happened. Normally, the machine brushes my hair a hundred times to keep it looking soft and silky. Today, the hairbrush decided to tangle my hair and pile it into a great big knot.

"Stop it!" I yelled.

But by now my hair was twisted on top of my head in the shape of a magpie's nest.

Before I could shout again, something even more strange happened: my crown began to fly.

Now you might think that this is just too stupid for words, and I must have imagined it.

But I didn't.

My crown sits on a silk cushion on a special table. There I was, gazing in horror at my new hairstyle, when I saw the cushion move. It sort of wobbled, like a plate of jelly. I stared at it. "Don't you dare..." I started.

The cushion was still for a moment, then it wobbled again. It seemed to sort of shrug my crown off into the air. I stared in disbelief. My best gold crown, set with diamonds, emeralds and pearls, rose up, hovered for a moment in mid-air, then came spinning towards me like a Frisbee.

"What...?"

I stared in horror as the crown whizzed through the air and landed on top of the bird's nest on my head.

"Look!" I commanded the empty air. "Just stop it!" I glared all round the room but everything was still.

Then I heard a tiny chuckle. I spun round swiftly.

No one there.

"Ha, ha, ha, haaaa."

The chuckle seemed to be escaping from my electric hairbrush. I glowered at its polished silver handle and its trailing wire and plug.

The hairbrush twitched.

"Don't you dare..."

The brush stifled another giggle and then it began to laugh out loud: "Ha ha ha haaaa."

It rocked from side to side. There was no doubt about it – the electric hairbrush was finding all this very amusing indeed.

I don't know how you would have felt if someone had told you there was a poltergeist in your bath.

I felt puzzled.

You see, I didn't know then what a poltergeist was. I looked up the word in my dictionary. It wasn't there. Then I looked up *haunt*. That wasn't there either.

Before I went to bed that night, I took out my silk-padded writing case and my best gold fountain pen. I removed a piece of parchment embossed with my royal crest and I wrote:

Dear Poltergeist,

Are you the same Pandora that's supposed to be lying behind the waterfall?
What does R.I.P. mean?
What do you want?

Her Most Royal Highness,
Princess Isobella

That was all I could think of to say to a poltergeist – whatever one was – so I just folded up the letter and placed it in a

parchment envelope. I melted a blob of
sealing wax and pressed it on the back with
my royal seal. On the front I wrote:

Pandora

and left it on my dressing-table.

Then I went to bed.

Chapter 3

The next morning, when I opened the lace curtains round my bed, I looked straight towards the envelope lying on my dressing-table. It was just where I'd left it last night.

Disappointed, I climbed out of bed and went to investigate. The seal on the envelope was unbroken but the name *Pandora* had been crossed out.

Underneath it, someone had written:

Isobella

but with no Royal Highness. What a cheek!

I turned the envelope over in my hand. There seemed no point in opening it. Pandora couldn't possibly have placed another letter inside – not without breaking the seal. Or could she?

I didn't know what poltergeists could do and what they couldn't. I decided to open it and see.

Inside the envelope was another piece of writing paper. I began to feel the goose pimples rise on my arm again. Something very strange was going on. I read:

Dear Isobella,

Yes I am the Same Pandora who lies
behind the Waterfall.
You really need to know about
life beyond the palace walls.
You need to know about Sickness
if you want to keep healthy. You
need to know about evil to
understand what it means to be
good. Most important, you need to
find out about death in order to
Stay alive. That's Why I'm haunting
you — I want you to know about the
danger you are in.
If you want to discover more,
you'll find the key hidden in
the mirror.
The quest demands courage,
curiosity and intelligence.
  love
  Pandora

P.S. Why do you call yourself Highness
When you are so very small?

Small, indeed! What a cheek! I felt tempted to screw up the letter and throw it away.

But I didn't.

I sat down and had a think.

I had been wondering for a long, long time about life beyond the palace walls. The only people to ask about it were the king and queen. I don't see them very often because they're too busy Ruling the Country. And when I do see them, they don't like answering questions.

One day at teatime, I plucked up courage, took a long, deep breath and asked my father: "What is there, Your Imperial Majesty, beyond the garden walls?"

The king paused with a forkful of chocolate truffle halfway to his mouth. There was a few moments' silence.

"There is nothing," the king told me slowly and – I thought – a little sadly. "There is nothing at all beyond the palace walls. This palace ... " he waved his arm around the

mirrored dining hall " ... and the garden –
that is all there is."

The queen replaced her diamond-cut
chalice of champagne on the glass-topped
table. "All," she added, "that you will ever
need to know."

I opened my mouth to argue, then changed
my mind. I don't know if you argue with your
parents. But when they're also the king and
queen, it's a rather different matter.

I stared down at my jelly, where my
distorted reflection wobbled back at me. I
knew they were lying. I knew they were lying
because of all the thousands of questions I
wanted to ask about the world beyond the
walls. They included things like:

• Where do all the servants live?

• What happens to the bathwater after it's
gone down the plughole?

• Where would the birds fly if we let them
out of the aviary?

And now, of course, added to the list:

• Who is Pandora?

- How can she lie behind the waterfall?
- Why am I in danger?
- And what is R.I.P.?

Back in my room, I walked across to the dressing-table and stared into the mirror.

"Mirror, mirror on the wall who's the fairest of them all?"

The mirror, as usual, said nothing. Not many keys to be found in there.

I decided to go out into the garden and inspect the waterfall again.

Chapter 4

The path to the waterfall led through rockeries and rose gardens. It passed by the glass aviary filled with brightly coloured birds and wound around the lake filled with brightly coloured fish.

The palace gardens are always perfect. The flowers fill the air with perfume; the birds trill on branches heavy with blossom. It is, as the king and queen have often told me, a kind of paradise.

So, why should I have this nagging need to find out about the world outside? Why should I fidget with frustration? Why should I feel like a prisoner?

Can a princess be a prisoner in paradise?

All I can say is that as I rushed towards the waterfall that morning, I felt an excitement that I'd never known before. My heart fluttered like the jewelled wings of a hummingbird. All my life I'd nursed the notion that there was another world out beyond the palace walls. Now I was going to find out.

When I reached the rockery, I clambered to the top, found the little wheel, rolled up my sleeves and turned the water off. Then I climbed down to the black stone slab.

"Pandora," I called softly.

No reply.

I inspected the rectangle of stone. It had a crack around the edge, just like a door but with no handle. I pushed but nothing happened. I pushed harder. Still, it wouldn't open. I was just about to leave, when I noticed something in the top corner: four rows of numbers.

The numbers were on buttons, exactly like the security keypads on the locked doors in the palace. I pressed the numbers at random. Nothing happened. I tried again. Still nothing.

I needed to find the key.

Back at the palace, I stared hard into my mirror.

All I could see was myself.

How could a mirror possibly hold a key?
Should I try to unscrew it and take it apart?
Might the key be hidden inside it somewhere?

"Mirror, mirror on the wall
who's the fairest of them all?"

I asked.
But as always the mirror said nothing.
I sighed. I slouched back to my bedroom
and lay on my bed. I pressed one of the story
buttons on my bedpost:

Once upon a time, there was a beautiful
princess...

Of course, I'd heard all the songs and
stories many times before. In fact, to tell you
the truth, I was starting to find them a bit of
a bore.

The princess will prick her finger on a spinning
wheel and get a nasty sore throat...

I pressed another button:

Jack and Jill went up the hill
  to fetch a pail of water
Jack fell down on an eiderdown...
  and Jill came tumbling after.

Nothing interesting ever happened to the people in the stories. Everybody had a nice time and they all lived happily ever after and that was it – the end. I sometimes wished that people would fall down when there wasn't a nice soft eiderdown to land on.

What would happen then?

Three kind mice, see how they run.
They all ran after the farmer's wife,
who cut them some cheese with a carving
  knife...

Boring. Boring. Boring.
I switched off the tape and went back to look at the mirror.

"Mirror, mirror on the wall
who's the fairest of them all...?"

Of course, the mirror, just for a change, said nothing.

So, once again, I examined it carefully. I ran my fingers along its gold, carved frame.

Nothing there.

I pushed the mirror away from the wall and searched behind it.

Still nothing.

But if nothing was there, how would I find the key?

Then I noticed the silver looking-glass lying on my dressing-table. I picked it up and turned it over. Of course, there was no key there either.

"Oh, boozle! Boozle! Boozle!"

I sat on the stool with my back to the dressing-table and wondered what to do next.

Just then, something caught my eye – a letter *𝒞*.

In my looking-glass, I could see the

reflection of the carved gold frame of my dressing-table mirror. Part of the carving looked like the letter T and ... yes, it was followed by a circle. My heart skipped a beat. The next bit was a swirly thing that might just be an F and then there was a little line and a dot and... I bounced up and down on my seat.

I held the looking-glass carefully and began to spell out: T–o F–i–n–d... I leapt in the air and landed back on my stool. This was the key! It had to be. I sprang off my seat and grabbed my writing case and fountain pen.

My fingers were shaking with excitement as I unscrewed the top of the pen. The letters had been there all the time. The key was in the mirror but hidden in mirror writing! Nobody could read it without looking in another mirror!

I figured out the letters and wrote them down carefully one by one. This is what they said:

To find the key to the waterfall
where Pandora is fairest of them all...

(Cheek! Just who did this Pandora think she was!)

Take the number of days that are in a year
and the number of mirrors in this room...

Well, it didn't take me long to work that out:
• the number of days in a year – three hundred and sixty five;
• the number of mirrors in my room – two.
So the number key must be:

3652

I rolled up my silken sleeve and wrote the number on my arm.
Then I deciphered the rest of the verse:

To find the key to the waterfall
where Pandora is fairest of them all...
Take the number of days that are in a year
and the number of mirrors in this room.
Unlock the doorway to a world of darkness ...
and descend the stairway
inside Pandora's tomb!

Chapter 5

I rushed through the rockeries and rose-scented archways. I sprinted round the summer house and skipped along the sun terrace. I couldn't wait to try the secret number and find the stairway inside Pandora's tomb.

Before leaving the palace, I had looked up *tomb* in my dictionary. I thought it should have been somewhere in between *tomato* and *tomcat* but it wasn't.

As I scurried round the ornamental lake, I did wonder why words like *tomb* and *poltergeist* and *haunt* weren't in my dictionary. Weren't they the right kind of words for a princess to include in her vocabulary? And did *tomb* rhyme with *comb*? Or with *room*? It sounded a bit like *gloom*.

I began to feel uneasy.

I strode past the tinkling fountains, whose spray formed rainbows in the sunlight, then I wondered about *The doorway to a world of darkness* – a place, presumably, that had no sun. It gave me a sense of dark storm clouds gathering. Why would anyone want to live there?

I walked more slowly.

What if there were reasons why the king and queen hadn't told me about the world beyond the palace walls? What if there was...? Of course, I didn't know what there could be – just a sense of deep fore-boding. A sense of something that came to me sometimes, like a long dark shadow in my dreams.

I stood still and paused for a moment. What if there was...?

But I couldn't think of anything to stop me. Now I'd got as far as this, I had to find out more. I had to unlock the doorway, even if it did lead to a world of darkness. And – even though I didn't know what I would meet when I got there – I had to descend the stairway inside Pandora's tomb.

So, I clambered up the rockery, rolled up my sleeve and checked the numbers. Then I reached up to the rectangular keypad in the corner of the stone. It had to be the right number.

Had to be.

3...6...5...2...

I took a deep breath then gave the big black stone a push. It seemed a bit loose. I pushed harder.

It opened!

I jumped up and down with excitement, nearly knocking off my crown. I glanced over my shoulder to check no one was watching, then I peered inside the door.

As you might expect, everything was gloomy.

I crouched down and took a small step inside.

The floor beneath my feet was hard as rock. I reached out my arms but there was no handrail. Just a slimy stone wall. I inched my way forward.

A ray of dim light from the doorway pierced the darkness. In its glow, I could see, standing on the floor, a large rectangular table. It seemed to be made of stone.

I was puzzled. The table didn't have a nice lace cloth and there were no chandeliers. It seemed a very odd place for anyone to eat their meal and I couldn't see any chairs.

I crept past the table.

Of course, I had seen darkness before – in the gardens at night; but then there was always a soft glow from the security lamps or from the moon and stars. Beyond the stone table there was only blackness. What if the door closed shut behind me? But then, I had my mobile phone – I could always call for the servants.

I stepped forward.

I waved my hands in front of my face but there was nothing to see. Just blackness.

I stepped further into the dark.

After only a few metres, the room stopped. There was a wall, but in the wall there was an opening. I reached my foot down and found a stair. Gingerly, I placed my foot on the stair and stepped downwards. I hesitated.

I could still see nothing in front of me, but I didn't want to turn back now. I reached my foot down again. There was another stair. Then another. *So*, I thought, as I stepped deeper and deeper, *this is the world of darkness and this must be the stairway inside Pandora's tomb*.

I turned the corner. I was clambering down a spiral staircase turning deeper and deeper underground. The air was heavy with a smell of damp and moss, rotting wood and empty rooms.

As I turned the second corner, I saw a tiny speck of light a long way down below. I wanted to run but I didn't. I clambered carefully step by step until I reached the opening. There wasn't a door this time, just an archway and daylight.

I walked through the archway, then stood and looked around.

My first impression was disappointment. There were some dirty, ramshackle buildings and a stony path. There were no flowers, no birds, no fountains or waterfalls and, to my great disappointment, no people.

I walked hesitantly down the path. I sniffed. There was a sickly smell of overripe fruit and dirty toilets. To my left, I could hear the rushing of a waterfall so that's the direction I took.

In between the old buildings was a tunnel, out of which a river flowed and tumbled. I walked on to the rickety wooden bridge that straddled the river, then stood and gazed at the water.

It was filthy.

In the palace gardens, the pools and fountains are always crystal clear. You can see right through the water to the multicoloured fish and glistening pebbles. Ripples skirt across the pools like pleats of silk. Rainbows shimmer where the sun shines through the spray of the waterfalls.

This water looked like liquid mud. It was gooey, gluey browny black. It had foul froth on top that didn't look like bubble bath. And the smell was ... ugh! I hate to have to tell you this, but the water actually smelled like ... well, like poo.

"Ugh!" I exclaimed.

I swallowed hard to stop myself being sick and, as I turned, I saw someone. Across the bridge was a girl, staring at me.

A royal princess, of course, does not expect to be stared at.

I stared back.

The girl didn't look away or curtsey; she just carried right on staring.

"Who are you?" I demanded.

The girl had been wheeling a wheelbarrow. She rested it on the ground and walked across the bridge towards me.

I was very shocked. Never in my life before had I seen anyone dressed like her. Instead of a nice silk dress, she wore silly little short trousers that showed her grubby knees. On her feet, instead of pretty embroidered sandals she wore boots. Yes – boots, the kind the palace gardeners wear. She wore a floppy, baggy shirt with a picture of a sort of juggling ball with some bits shaded in.

One World

it said in squiggly writing.

But the most disgusting thing about this creature was her hair. Mine, of course, is brushed a hundred times a day. This grumbleweed looked as though hers hadn't been brushed a hundred times in her life. It was so short at the front she might have been going bald, then it was scrunched at the back and sides into ragged bunches of plaits – like rats' tails.

And she had the cheek to stroll towards me and hold out her grubby little paw for me to shake. "Hi, Isobella," she said. She didn't even call me Royal Highness.

I pulled a face.

"I'm really pleased to meet you," she continued, undeterred. "I'm Pandora. Your sister."

Chapter 6

Chapter 6

Of course, I just turned and ran. I clambered back over the bridge and through the arch. Then I lifted my long silk skirt and pounded up the spiral staircase, holding my head straight to stop my crown from falling off. Thankfully, the door at the top was still open. I squeezed through, then slammed it tightly closed behind me. I turned on the waterfall and sprinted straight back to the palace. Back in my private rooms, I stepped out of my muddy dress and plunged into a steamy, hot, perfumed bath.

"How dare she!" I exclaimed, squirting strawberry bubble bath out of the dispenser.

"How dare she!" I repeated, taking a nice long drink of chocolate milkshake.

"She can't possibly be my sister!" I lay back in the bubbles. "She's so dirty and messy and..." I shuddered as I remembered her plaited hair and wheelbarrow full of dirt. "Ugh!"

Obviously, if I did have a sister, my parents would have told me. They wouldn't just not mention it and wait for me to bump into her one day when I was half grown-up.

I did realize though, as I squirted myself another milkshake, that the only thing for me to do was ask them.

"Could you tell me please, Your Imperial Majesty," I asked the king as he tucked into his coconut cream sundae, "who Pandora is?"

The king turned pale.

I glanced at the queen, who was gazing in horror at her embroidered napkin and twisting it into knots.

The silence echoed between the three of us. It reflected around the mirrored walls. It froze into sudden stillness, the orange flames flickering on the crystal chandeliers.

The king replaced his fork on his silver plate.

The queen opened her mouth. "There's no such—"

But the king interrupted. "Pandora is a young woman in a story," he swallowed hard, "who lived a long time ago. She had a box which she had been warned not to open. Although Pandora already had everything she wanted, she was overcome with curiosity. She had to find out what was in the box."

There was another long pause.

"So Pandora isn't ... real?"

The king shook his head.

"Well, could you please tell me ..." I hesitated, because I knew that this would give my discovery away, "... what is meant by R.I.P.?"

The blood seemed to drain completely from the queen's face. Her skin turned as pale as the inside of a coconut. She began to slither slowly from her golden throne down towards the floor.

I thought at first that the king said *the rest is in pieces* as Her Imperial Majesty disappeared rapidly from sight, but he didn't. The words he spoke were *Rest in Peace* as he called for the servants to come and pick up the queen.

* * *

So, Hansel and Gretel went inside the nice old lady's gingerbread cottage. The sweet old lady gave them barley sugar and gingerbread and iced biscuits and lots of orange juice ...

I knew the king and queen were lying. I knew I'd met a person called Pandora. I didn't know whether she was a poltergeist or not because I still hadn't found out what a poltergeist was.

... when Hansel and Gretel were full up, the nice old lady gave them some sweets and biscuits in a bag to take back home. When they explained that they were lost, she took out a large map and showed them the way back to their cottage ...

I lay awake and wondered. Why should the stone say "Here lies Pandora" when Pandora was standing up? Why did it say "Rest in Peace"? And why was Pandora warned not to open the box? What could have been hidden inside?

... so they ran skipping through the forest, back home to their father and their nice new stepmother.

Boring, boring, boring. I reached out and switched off the story tape.

Why did everybody in stories always have to live happily ever after? What was the point in listening to a story if you knew that everything would always turn out right in the end?

But what else could happen? How could things not turn out all right?

I wondered if things had perhaps not turned out right for Pandora.

I was determined to find out.

Chapter 7

The next time I went back down the spiral staircase, I decided to explore.

I tiptoed through the archway at the foot of the steps, then stood and peered around. There was nobody about. I crept along the path to the first large wooden shed. I could hear the gushing of the dirty waterfall, but there was still no birdsong, no footsteps and no voices.

The door of the shed was closed.

Very quietly, I lifted the latch. I tried to peep inside, but the shed was too dark. I opened the door.

At first, I could see nothing. I stepped inside. As my eyes became accustomed to the gloom, I could see that there were wooden shelves all the way along the walls. Standing on the shelves were rows and rows of square glass boxes.

I looked all around. The room was very still. There was a low hum like a waterfall pump. I stepped towards the nearest glass box, lit by a sliver of light from the half-open door. It seemed to be nothing but a tankful of dirty water. I screwed up my eyes and peered closer. Floating inside was what looked like a large, fat creature with lots of heads and fins. Then my stomach turned over as I realized it was actually a clump of goldfish, squashed so tightly that at first they seemed like a multi-headed blob.

The fish gazed at me with round, wide eyes through the green slime of the glass, opening and closing their mouths as if they were panting for breath. They dangled vertically in the water, with no room to flap their fins and no room to turn around.

My heart beat against my ribs as I shuffled past the rows of grimy tanks. Each one was just as dark and slimy as the next and each held a different kind of gasping, stifled fish. I stared back, as open-mouthed as the fish. Why weren't the fish outside, swimming in nice, clear pools? Why were their tanks so small? Why were so many of them kept here in the dark?

I explored the rest of the shed but there was nothing else to see. Just row upon row of fish, each one staring at me with its round, sad, soulful eyes.

I walked back out of the shed and fastened the door behind me.

"Now would you like to see the birds?"

I jumped. I hadn't noticed the old woman standing beside the door.

"Come along. I'll show you." She pointed at the second wooden shed.

I turned towards her. She had a dirty, wrinkled face and wore a long black cloak with her head covered by a black hood. On her feet, she wore boots – just like Pandora's.

I didn't know what to say.

In the palace gardens, our birds are kept in a beautiful aviary with a tall glass roof. The jewelled hummingbirds hover in between the multicoloured tropical plants; kingfishers and yellow wagtails bob and skim through the waterfalls.

"Come along."

The wooden shed didn't look a suitable place for an aviary but I did want to explore. I turned and followed the strange woman.

Now, if you find the idea of a shed full of squashed fish disturbing, I can tell you that a shed full of squashed birds is even worse.

"Hope is here; Hope is at hand;
Hope for breakfast; Hope for tea..."

screeched a parrot in the corner.

I hurried past the rows of dreary cages where cramped and clustered birds didn't even have room to spread their wings. I peered through the darkness at kingfishers and wagtails, hummingbirds and canaries, budgies, parrots and chaffinches – all caged inside the wire mesh, where they could only dream of blue skies, sunshine and rainbows.

Hope is here; Hope is at hand
Hope for breakfast; Hope for tea...

My heart felt even tighter, pressing against my ribs. "I don't want to stay here any longer!" I exclaimed. "Can't you look after the poor creatures better than this?"

The old woman took a deep breath. "I do the best I can," she answered, "but there are so many birds and fish and so few hours in a day." She paused. "And the king and queen refuse to allow anyone else to come down here and help me."

Of course, I didn't understand her.

I turned to leave. Just as I reached the door, however, I heard a familiar voice call out, "But these are *your* birds, Isobella ..."

I spun around.

"... and *your* fish."

Suddenly, appearing from nowhere, was scabby Pandora with her scraggy hair and wheelbarrow full of dirt.

"It's because of you that the birds and fish are kept like this."

I felt like slapping her horrid, grubby face.

"So what are you going to do?"

* * *

I stuck my nose high in the air and marched straight past Pandora, two of my fingers squeezing my nostrils tightly to show how smelly I thought she was.

I stamped on to the rickety bridge and gazed down at the swirling water.

"Be careful. That bridge isn't very strong."

I raised my foot and stamped it down really hard, just to show how much notice I was taking.

Pandora walked on to the bridge behind me.

I felt very tempted to storm up the spiral staircase and march straight back to my nice comfortable palace but now, of course, I had a lot more questions to ask. If I ran straight home, I wouldn't have the chance to find out anything at all.

I took a deep breath and turned to face Pandora. "They're not my fish," I insisted, "and they're not my birds either. So why did you say they were?"

"They're the spare birds and fish. If

anything should happen to the birds and fish in your lovely palace gardens, then they'd be replaced with one of these."

I didn't believe her. "Well, what could happen?"

Pandora hesitated. "They might ... they might ... die."

Dye?

I didn't think that was very likely. I'd never known a bird or fish suddenly change colour before. And if they did, it wouldn't matter.

"Well, what happens if these birds and fish aren't needed? What if they never have to replace anything?"

Pandora looked sad as she took a step towards me. "Then they stay in the sheds until they die."

I moved swiftly away. I didn't want her standing next to me. I wanted to argue with her, but how could I tell her she was stupid when I didn't even understand what she meant?

I gazed at the murky water and decided to

change the subject. "Why don't you clean the waterfall?" I complained. "Why do you let it get so dirty?"

Pandora gazed around. "All this underworld exists just to keep you in your life of luxury." She pointed to the sick-coloured, smelly froth and pieces of yellow tissue floating by. "That's *your* water, Isobella – the water from your sink and from your bath and toilet. You see," she pointed, "you've been using strawberry bubble bath and bright yellow tissue today. Yesterday it was orange."

I gasped out loud. There are certain things that should never be discussed in public. And a royal princess's dirty bathwater and the contents of her toilet are two of them. "How dare you!" I raised my foot and stamped it down hard.

"Be careful!"

The bridge made a splintering sound. "Shut up, sausage-brain!"

I stumbled forward as the boards beneath my feet gave way. I tried to grab the handrail but fell to my knees.

Pandora reached out her hand but I shrugged it away. "Don't touch me! You stupid boozle!"

I reached for the *S* on my mobile phone, but before I could press the button, I found myself falling straight through the broken boards. The phone flew out of my hand.

"Help!"

I reached out to grab Pandora's hand too late as I began to tumble down towards the filthy, swirling water.

Chapter 8

The only water I'd ever been in before was my nice, hot, bubble bath.

This was totally different.

For a start, the river was icy cold. As soon as I hit the water, I screamed out loud, then the dirty horrid scum filled my mouth and I couldn't scream any more.

The river swept me away, dashing my arms and legs against the rocks. Sharp stones grazed and stung me. Then, as the water grew more still, it dragged me down deeper and deeper, filling my eyes and nose and throat. "Help!" I tried to shout, but as I opened my mouth, it filled with water again. I felt frightened. I couldn't breathe; I couldn't speak and I couldn't see anything but mud.

"Isobella!" I heard someone shout. "Try to swim!"

I didn't know how to swim but it suddenly seemed a good idea to learn. I thought it might be best to learn quite quickly.

I splashed my arms and legs from side to side like a frog. At first I just sank deeper and deeper, but then my head popped out of the water and I was able to take a breath.

"That's it! Grab my hand!"

I stretched out my arm and someone dragged me towards the bank. "Come on, Isobella. Put your feet down. Try and walk."

I stretched my feet towards the slippery rocks and found that I could stand.

"Come on!"

I staggered forward. My mouth and eyes and nose and throat were full of slime and I was panting and gasping for breath. Then, as someone wrapped their arms around me, I stumbled and fell.

When I opened my eyes, I was lying on something nice and soft, but I certainly wasn't being driven around the grounds by my chauffeur in my personal limousine. In fact, it felt more as if I was being bumped along on a tea trolley. There was a nasty smell as well. I closed my eyes.

"We found her lying in a wheelbarrow,

Your Majesty."

"What?!"

"Sitting on a pile of manure."

"What?!"

"Her clothes looked as though she'd – well, as though she'd fallen in a sewer."

"Send for a doctor."

The voices sounded a long, long way off.

"What *have* you been doing, Isobella?"

When I opened my eyes, everything swirled around in circles. I thought it best to keep them closed. I shivered with cold, even though I was now wrapped tightly in a cocoon of woolly blankets.

"Carry her upstairs!"

I woke up to find a long rubber tube being forced inside my nose. "Aaaaaaaagh!" I screamed and tore it out. When someone tried to hold me down, I punched out with my fists and when that didn't stop them, I kicked them on the shin.

"Isobella. Look at me."

Standing in front of me, rubbing her leg, was the old woman with the long black cloak. "Do you remember me?"

I said nothing.

"My name's Hope. You saw me looking after the birds. Your parents have sent for me to try to make you better."

I still said nothing.

"Did you swallow water from the river?"

I nodded.

"That water is poisonous. It will kill you. That's why we have to pump out your stomach."

I shook my head in horror.

"We're trying to save your life, Isobella. If we don't do this, you'll die. It's going to hurt but we can't do it if you keep fighting."

I closed my eyes and fell back on the pillow.

I don't know how long I spent asleep after my unspeakable ordeal. I kept hearing voices and seeing faces round my bed but I don't know which were real and which were part of my nightmare. I remember several times thinking that the pain was too much to bear and wanting to go to sleep and never wake up again. Each time I thought that though, I heard someone call out my name. And when I opened my eyes, there was Hope, holding tightly to my hand.

Chapter 9

"Is this where she sleeps?"

I opened my eyes when I heard the king and queen climbing the stairs to my room.

"It's this door here, Your Majesty."

Although my eyes were open, I had a strange feeling of not being completely there. It wasn't just that I was half-asleep; I felt that part of me – the bit that makes me Isobella – was hovering somewhere in between my body and the ceiling.

The king scooped up his fur-lined robe, then squatted on the low stool by my bed. His face was red with the effort of climbing the stairs. "How did you find the river?" he asked crossly.

I felt very weak. It was hard for me to find the strength to think. It was even harder to find the strength to explain about Pandora.

"Were you kidnapped?"

At the foot of the bed was my dressing-table. Reflected in its mirror was the queen, rearranging her hair as she sat upon my padded stool.

"Well...?"

I struggled to remember. "I found Pandora's tomb," I explained. But as I spoke the dreaded name, I heard a gasp of horror. I looked up towards the mirror and saw the colour draining once again from Her Imperial Majesty's face.

"I opened the door in the tomb and walked through – down the steps."

The king opened his eyes wide. His face became even redder. "But, Isobella, there is no tomb. No staircase and no door. And ..." his voice trembled slightly, "... I've told you before ... Pandora is just a person in a story."

Her Imperial Majesty's complexion was now as pale as the petal of a water lily. Through my feverish haze, I became aware of her slow slithering from my padded stool, down towards the floor.

"The key was in the mirror," I explained. But then, when I looked at the mirror, of course there was nothing there. Just a fancy scroll around the edges. No letters.

No words. No secret writing. Just Her Imperial Majesty, sliding lower and lower like a rapidly melting ice-cream cornet.

Then everything turned fuzzy. The room began to hum. Beads of sweat dripped off my face and onto my silken bedspread.

But before the king could notice, his attention was distracted by the queen's gold crown as it rolled across the carpet. The queen had slumped right down to the floor before the servants could pick her up.

My body was bathed in sweat. I felt as if my forehead was on fire. I kept reaching out to press my hand on the wall and on the bedposts, searching for something cool. The next thing I knew, I was shivering. I felt so cold that my teeth chattered. I had to call out for the servants to bring me even more blankets and a hot water bottle.

I remember waking in the night and seeing a sliver of sky through the narrow gap in my bedroom curtains. As I gazed at the stars, sparkling in the blackness, I remembered Pandora and her wheelbarrow. Was she the one who had rescued me from the river?

I don't know whether I was dreaming or not when I called out Pandora's name. I do remember her talking to me, just as though she were sitting at my bedside. "Perhaps you can understand now, Isobella," she explained, "why I had to come back and haunt you. When you didn't understand about death, you were in danger all the time. There were all kinds of things you might do to harm yourself." She dabbed at my forehead with the sheet. "None of us knows how precious life can be until we see it slip away."

"Was that what was happening in the river? Was that my life being dragged down and swept away?"

Pandora squeezed my hand tightly.

"You see, Pandora," I struggled to explain, "I'm beginning to think there are lots of questions I need to ask you."

I opened my eyes and there she was,

kneeling beside me, bathed in moonlight, holding my hand in hers. "We can talk when you get better," she insisted. "First of all, you need to rest. Rest and sleep."

"How long will you be here, though?"

"Until you get properly better."

I remember feeling very, very weak. I wanted to cry but I couldn't find the energy. "What shall I do if I want to talk to you?"

Pandora squeezed my hand tightly between hers. "Just call out my name."

Chapter 10

The next time I ventured down the spiral staircase, it was in the middle of the night.

This time, there was no light behind me and I knew that when I descended the steep stairs, there would be no welcoming glow shining through the arch.

However, I thought, as I placed my new sturdy boot on the first of the slippery steps, I now knew where I was going and what I had to do.

I wasn't sure how long I'd been ill but now I was feeling stronger.

Strong enough to carry out my plan.

At the foot of the staircase was the arch. I couldn't see it but I knew it was there. I stood on the bottom step and called softly, "Pandora!"

Before long, I heard the rumbling of a wheelbarrow, and there she was, standing right beside me. "Right then," she said. "Are we set?"

We began to walk along the path together side by side.

When I had realized Pandora really was my sister – and therefore, a princess as well – I lent her a spare crown, one of my second-best ones. It was a sort of headband covered in diamonds which sparkled as she walked so I could actually see her in the dark.

While I was ill, Pandora had visited me in my private rooms. Needless to say, I'd offered her the full use of my facilities and now she smelt less of manure and more of bubble bath and soap.

When I started feeling well enough to go outside, we began to practise our juggling together in the palace gardens. We discovered that although each of us found it hard to juggle more than two balls at once, between the two of us we could actually juggle three or four together.

"Pandora," I asked as we trundled the wheelbarrow together in the darkness, "did you enjoy being a princess?"

The moon appeared from behind the

clouds and lit the path towards the first wooden shed.

"Well, I did and I didn't," said Pandora. "The king and queen wanted me to be good. They wanted me to be sweet and innocent. They thought that because they were so powerful they could stop me finding out about all the bad things in life. They never told me about illness, poverty or old age. They certainly never talked to me about death."

"That's just like me."

"But then I discovered all the troubles in the world, all in a single day – well, less than that – within an hour. It was too much for me to cope with."

We parked our wheelbarrow next to the shed and Pandora opened the door.

"So how did you find out?"

"I used to feel very lonely," she explained as we lifted the wheelbarrow into the shed. I didn't have anyone to talk to or play with so I started reading books. The characters in the books were like friends to me."

"But the stories I have are so boring!"

Pandora walked towards the wooden shelf and lifted down the first tankful of fish.

"Well, I read proper stories about people who had adventures, who got lost in the forest and were eaten up by giants. Stories about monsters and witches and poor people who didn't live in palaces." She positioned the tank squarely inside the barrow. "Once I found out there were other people living beyond the palace walls, I had to go out and meet them."

I stared down at the tankful of swishing fish. "So, the stories have all been altered. Everything has been rewritten."

Pandora looked up at me. I couldn't see her face in the dark but there was sadness in her voice. "That's right. They were hiding the truth from you. They did it because they were frightened." She placed her hand briefly on my arm. "They were frightened of facing up to all the bad things in the world. They were hiding the truth from themselves."

Both of us together lifted down the next tank of fish and placed it in the barrow.

"What I still can't understand, though," I said, "is why the king and queen never wanted me to know about you."

"Well," Pandora answered, sliding the two tanks together, "instead of stopping at home and being sad when I died, instead of saying nice things about me, they just carried on Ruling the Country."

I gasped in horror. "You mean, just as if nothing had happened? Just as if they weren't bothered?"

Pandora reached down another tank of fish. "I don't think that was the reason. I think they just found it really hard to accept what had happened. They'd always assumed that because they had so much money, they could have anything they wanted. They thought they could control everything in the world. And now they'd encountered something that their power could not control.

Of course, it was too much for them to cope with. They just prayed for another daughter to be born as soon as possible."

I lifted down some more tanks until we'd lined the bottom of the barrow. "So they thought of me as a replacement, then. Like the fish and the birds."

Pandora grinned. "Well, you could say that, although we're not exactly similar. But, you see, when *you* were born," she began placing more tanks sideways across the first layer, "the king and queen built the palace walls even higher. They employed Hope to work in the gardens. Then, if any of the birds or fish looked ill, she had to change them over quickly before you noticed. In that way, they would never have to explain to you about illness or about death.

" Next they destroyed the books and had different versions of the songs and stories put on tape. Only then could they be certain you would grow up in a world where there was only goodness, where you would never find out about evil or death."

We completed the second row of tanks. "Where I would know only boredom," I added.

Pandora nodded as she placed a big cover across the fish. "Just tell me about it," she said.

Chapter 11

I don't know if you've ever had to carry a wheelbarrowful of squashed fish up a spiral staircase in the dark but, believe me, it isn't easy.

Fortunately, Pandora had lent me a pair of trousers, some of her second-best, she said. I was relieved to find that they came down to my ankles. (I really don't think a princess should show her knees in public, even in the dark.) Just like my new sturdy boots, I found the trousers very useful when I was clambering up the staircase with the fish.

"Let's leave them here till we've fetched the others," suggested Pandora when we arrived at the lake.

So, we lifted the tanks out of the wheelbarrow and set them out in a row.

Now, you may not be surprised to hear that this was the first time in my life that I'd done any proper work – the first time I'd ever felt really tired. I did think it might kill me (now I was beginning to understand that people don't just go on for ever) but to my amazement, I found it fun. In fact, it was probably the happiest day of my life.

The two of us rested by the lake and watched the moonlight sparkling on the water. Then it was time to go back with the barrow and reload.

I can't remember how many times we clambered up and down the staircase. We had to be careful, because, if you drop a tank of fish on a staircase in the dark, it isn't easy to pick them up. And as far as I know, we didn't drop a single fish.

We lifted out the very last tank and stood it beside the lake.

"What I think we should do," said Pandora, "is submerge the tanks inside the water and let the fish swim out when they want. The water in the tanks will be warmer than the lake. If they fall from a great height into icy-cold water, they might get a nasty shock."

"I know," I said. "Just tell me about it."

* * *

Well, if you think that liberating a whole shedful of overcrowded fish sounds exciting, what about liberating a shedful of overcrowded birds?

I had assumed that the birds would fly up the stairs by themselves. "Why do we have to carry them," I asked, "when they've got wings?"

Pandora shook her head sadly. "They may have wings," she explained, "but that doesn't mean they can fly. If you've been imprisoned in a cage, it might make you afraid of the world outside. It would be cruel just to let them out and leave them. They need us to help them along."

So, we rumbled the wheelbarrow back to the aviary and began to load up the birds.

I felt exhausted but also happier than I'd ever been before. I suppose you might say that having discovered how near death can be, I now knew what it meant to be truly alive.

The cages were lighter than the fish tanks.

Also, we weren't so frightened of dropping them, so we were able to pile quite a lot together on the barrow. So many, in fact, that I completely lost sight of Pandora. All I could see, as I staggered for the first time up the staircase, was a sad owl, a cluster of kingfishers and a parrot that kept squawking:

> *"Hope is here! Hope is at hand!*
> *Hope for breakfast. Hope for tea.*
> *Hope might still be left behind*
> *but rather her than me!"*

When we'd finished, I sat down with Pandora in the aviary. It had always been my favourite spot. I loved the heady scent of the tropical flowers and the wispy shapes of ferns. I enjoyed the warmth and special greenhouse smell.

As I was saying, it had been the happiest day – or should I say night – of my life, but I had a feeling now that something was ending. I was fearful that once we'd liberated all the birds, Pandora might want to leave.

I tried to think very quickly whether there was anything else I needed to ask her. "About death…" I started.

"Mmm?" Pandora came and sat next to me under a palm tree.

"Why do people have to die?"

She thought for a moment. "Because if they didn't, the world would get full up." She glanced down at the cage of kingfishers squashed against their wire mesh. "There would be far too many people squashed in too small a space. There would be no room for any new babies and people would just get older and older."

I thought about that for a moment. "But it's not only old people that die, though, is it? I mean, you weren't old, Pandora…"

She nodded. "People can die from all kinds of things. As you've found out, Isobella, they can drown; they can be poisoned; they can fall; they can catch a terrible disease… Life doesn't come with any guarantees. Any of us can die at any time.

"The only thing we can be sure of is that if we haven't died by the time we get old, we'll die then. No one goes on for ever."

I thought about that as well. "And what happens then?" I asked. "You make it sound as though when you die, everything just stops. But you haven't just stopped."

Pandora opened the door of the nearest cage. She allowed a hummingbird to hop on to her finger. "Most things in life," she said softly, "turn around in circles: winter and summer, night and day, rain and sun. Most things seem to disappear, then they come back – and each time they're a little bit different. Spring always follows winter but every spring is different from the last. Day always follows night, but every day is different. So," she explained, "it would make sense to me if life goes round just like everything else."

I nodded.

I thought for a moment, then realized the

question I'd been wanting to ask her all the time. "What's it like though?" I said at last. "I mean, what's it like being…"

Pandora held the hummingbird close to her and stroked its jewelled wings. "Our bodies are only a cage," she said. Her voice was as gentle as a feather. "So when you die, it's just like somebody opening the door of your cage and setting your spirit free."

I nodded.

Then I reached across and opened the door of a cage.

The next day, I went back on my own and sat inside the aviary. I'd brought some pieces of toast with me and some nuts. I spread them around on the floor and sat as still as a soap dish, waiting for the birds.

I had intended calling out Pandora's name but then I changed my mind. I thought that perhaps now I was better and now the birds and fish were free, she might not want to come back any more.

I had enjoyed meeting her. I'd enjoyed talking to her and juggling with her but I was thinking that now I knew about the world beyond the palace walls, perhaps it was time for me to find a proper friend.

I mean, what kind of friend is a ghost?

First of all, the chaffinches hopped down for bits of toast, then a blue budgie perching on a low branch pecked at the nuts. Then a hummingbird flew down and hovered by my face.

I took out some tiny little crumbs of toast and spread them on my palm. The aviary had always seemed like a paradise to me, a paradise built for birds. But now I'd learnt that nobody can build a paradise for someone else. You can't have a paradise with high walls round it. It *is* possible for a princess to be a prisoner in paradise, because in order to live in paradise, first of all you have to be free.

The jewelled hummingbird perched for a second on the finger of my outstretched hand.

Its tiny beady eye looked knowingly at me for a moment, then it pecked at the crumbs and flew away.

THE STONE THAT GREW

Enid Richemont

Is it magic? Is it alien? Katie's got a stone that grows!

Katie finds the stone in an old box in the loft. She thinks it's wonderful – and she's not going to share it, like she has to share her mum with her little stepbrother, Jake. It might even be a way of getting in with Sarah and her gang. Meanwhile, the stone just grows and grows... Where will it all end?

"With short chapters and lively dialogue, an easy-to-manage novel with an intriguing story." *The Guardian*

"Very well written... An excellent, thought-provoking book." *The School Librarian*

HAUNTED HOUSE BLUES

Theresa Tomlinson

Danny and Sally come across the house by accident, hidden among thick brambles. It's very old and grand but in a real mess, its wonderful stone carvings covered in spray paint. There's something sad and lonely about the place that makes Danny want to sit down and play the blues on his harmonica. But why does Mad Mason, the school caretaker, have such an interest in the house? How long can Danny and Sally keep it safe from Gary Fox and his gang? Who is the boy waving at the turret-room window? Past and present overlap intriguingly in this absorbing story.

MORE WALKER PAPERBACKS
For You to Enjoy

Name _____

Address _____

_____